Sing, Sing, Midnight!

By Emily Ridge Gallagher

Illustrations by R.B. Pollock & Emily Ridge Gallagher

Dedicated to Robbie, and to all the men, women, and kids whose families are separated by fences and who choose to love anyway.

Special thanks to all of the pre-readers, inside and out, who helped shape Maya and Midnight's journey.

Special thanks to my parents who supported this project and its author throughout.

For more information please email singsingmidnight@gmail.com or visit our website Singsingmidnight.com

ISBN:1533246106
ISBN-13: 978-1533246103

I am so excited because tomorrow it will be Saturday, my favorite day of the week. On Saturdays we go on a train trip to visit my Daddy.

My Daddy lives in a prison. Prison is where grownups go when they've made a bad choice and get into trouble. It's kind of like time-out. I hate time-out. My Daddy made a bad choice, but I still love him very much.

Mommy comes to kiss me goodnight and tuck me into bed. I'm very excited about our trip—WAY too excited to sleep! I'd rather wiggle. Mommy rubs my back to help me calm down.

"Who takes care of Daddy in prison?" I ask, stalling so she doesn't stop rubbing my back. "You should ask him tomorrow, Maya," she says. Then she tickles my feet and turns out the light.

We have to get on the train very early, before the sun even wakes up! I like to wave to people on boats as we go by.

My little brother, Stefan, snores in my Mommy's arms. He's still a baby and likes to sleep most of the time. Mommy says he'll be more fun when he's older. I'm not so sure.

When we get to the prison, an officer signs us in. Then we empty our pockets, take off our shoes, and go through a metal detector.

I used to be afraid of the officers but Mommy told me they are there to keep us safe.

We go through a big metal door into the visit room. Chairs and tables are lined up in long rows, just like on the train. An officer tells us which table is ours and then we wait for...

...DADDY!!!

We hug and kiss Daddy.
"Maya, have you gotten taller since I last saw you?"
He always asks me that.

"No, but I lost a tooth!"
"Wow! You are growing up fast, Kiddo!"

We all sit around our table and I *finally* get to ask my question.
"Daddy, who takes care of you in here?"

"Well, the officers keep me safe."
I already knew that.
"But who keeps you company?"

"I have friends. We play
cards, tell jokes, and make
music together."

"Okay, okay, but who tucks you in and tickles your feet
and kisses you goodnight?"

"Oh, well there isn't really anyone who does all that.
But, when I get really lonely, there's always Midnight."

I wonder how a cat got to prison. "Did Midnight make a bad choice?"

"Oh, no, Kiddo. Midnight *decided* to live here. Come sit with me and I'll tell you the story, just the way I heard it."

There was once a little orange kitten who lived in a box . He had two brothers and two sisters but no name yet. There was never enough room in the box for him to stretch out, but he was warm, and safe, and very curious.

People say curiosity and cats don't mix, and that's probably true. Sometimes curiosity has consequences. The kitten didn't care about the consequences; he loved going on adventures all by himself.

He wanted to see what the world had to offer. He wandered far and wide, exploring dumpsters and chasing mice and birds and leaves blowing in the wind. He loved coming home and telling his brothers and sisters about his travels.

One day, he returned to his box with a great story about a cricket he'd chased, but his brothers and sisters were gone. He meowed and howled for them, but they didn't answer.

A bird heard him crying and flew over to tell him that a nice lady had taken them home with her.
"Why did she take them away?" the kitten wondered.
"She said that she wanted them to come live with her family," the bird said.
"Everybody needs a family."

That night, alone in the box that suddenly felt much too big, Midnight shivered and wished he hadn't gone off by himself. He wondered whether he could make things right and whether he would ever be part of a family again.

"Daddy, I think this is a sad story."
"Don't worry, kiddo. It's only a sad start."

The next morning, the kitten was hungry and lonely, so he walked down to the river in search of food and a family. He watched some fishermen down by the water. "Maybe *they* could be my family!"

When he got closer, he saw they already had a mean old cat who did not look like she was in the mood to share her breakfast, or her family.

There was a hotdog stand nearby, and the kitten tried to use his charm to get some food. The man with the cart scratched him behind the ears, but didn't offer anything to eat.

Soon, a truck pulled up. A man got out and headed to the hotdog stand to get his lunch.

The man's truck smelled like all kinds of food— burgers and hotdogs and egg sandwiches— so the kitten jumped in to see if he could find a snack.

Unfortunately all he found were wrappers. The back of the truck was messy but warm from the sun; so the kitten curled up in a toolbox and took a nap.

A few minutes later, the truck started moving. The kitten started to feel excited, and a little scared.

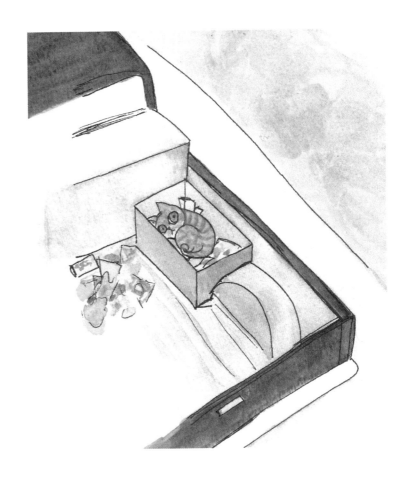

When the truck stopped, the man got out of the truck and reached for his toolbox.
"Well, who do we have here?" the man asked. "Listen, I don't know where you came from, but I've got work to do and can't have a kitten getting in the way."
He set the kitten down and walked away.

"What is this place?" wondered the kitten. There were high walls and gates, and lots and lots of men. Some played cards, others talked on the phone, a few were taking showers — outside!

One man noticed the kitten and offered him a small piece of beef jerky. Soon, the kitten was getting lots of attention. Guys lined up to scratch behind his ears and offer him treats. "I think I like it here," the kitten thought.

The sun went down and a loud voice instructed all the men to clear out of the yard. The kitten decided to follow.

They walked a long way, up and down hills, until they reached a large building. Inside the building, each man had his own room, with bars instead of doors.

The kitten liked the bars because he could slip between them and visit whoever he wanted.

On the first night, a man named Joe was having a hard time falling asleep. It was his daughter's birthday and he missed her very much.

The kitten missed his family too. He hopped up on Joe's bed and snuggled beside him. They both fell asleep quickly and had wonderful dreams of family.

The kitten loved exploring the prison. It was enormous! There were lots of new places to discover.

There were groundhogs and birds to play with too!

He played nicely and let them get away so he could play with them again another day.

The kitten was always careful not to wander too far away from his new friends. He had learned his lesson.

After a few days, the kitten began to learn more about the men. Some men played games with string or balls, and he got his exercise with them.

Some men shared tuna or sardines with him. He purred, rubbed their feet with his head while they ate, and came running whenever he heard a can open.

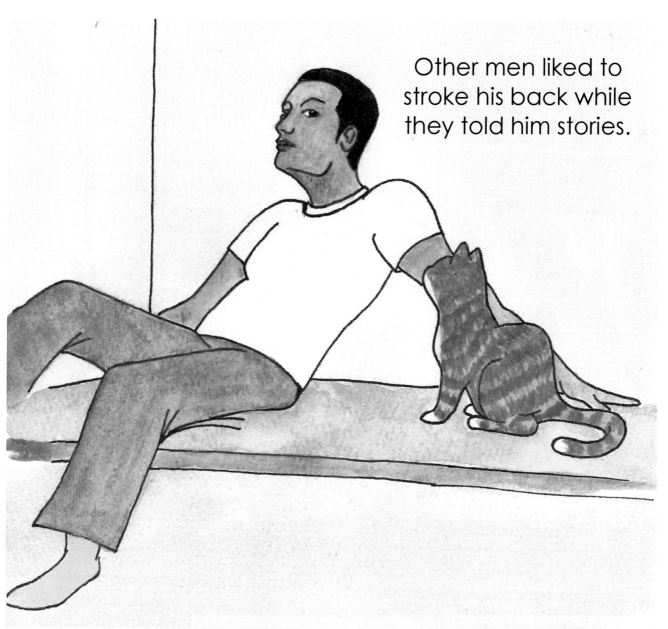

Other men liked to stroke his back while they told him stories.

Some scratched his ears while they wrote letters to their friends and kids.

But more than anything else, the kitten loved singing along whenever someone played music.

The men played guitar and sang beautiful songs and the kitten meowed, howled, and screeched along. One night, as he sang, someone yelled, "C'mon man! It's midnight!"

The man with the guitar yelled back, "It sure is! *Midnight's the best singer around!*"

From that day forward, the little orange kitten was known as Midnight.

Soon, Midnight became a part of prison life.

The librarian bought him a litter box, which he *really* appreciated.

One of the officers gave him a collar with his name on a silver tag.

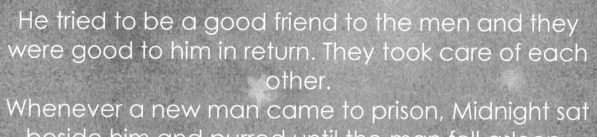

He tried to be a good friend to the men and they were good to him in return. They took care of each other.
Whenever a new man came to prison, Midnight sat beside him and purred until the man fell asleep.
He remembered how scary it had been to be alone, far away from his family, and he tried to comfort his new friends.

One morning, after filling up on breakfast and ear scratches, Midnight went outside to warm himself in the sun. He looked at the high walls of the prison and the faces of the men he had come to love. He purred and thought, "I am finally home. This is my family now."

"You were right, Daddy, that was not a sad story."
"Only a sad start," he said.
He stroked my hair and smiled at me and Mommy.
Stefan had fallen asleep again in Mommy's arms.
I held Daddy's hand.

"Do you ever get lonely, Daddy?" I asked.
"Sure, I do. I miss you, and your Mommy, and your brother, every day. But I'm learning how to make good choices so I can be the best Daddy I can be. Don't you worry though, Kiddo. Midnight takes good care of me."

As we left the prison, I started feeling very sad.
I already missed my Daddy so much.

Then, I felt something brush against my legs.

It was a little orange cat! Could it be Midnight??

I scratched his head and asked him to take good care
of my Daddy. I know he will.

Made in the USA
Columbia, SC
20 June 2019